The Salem Academy for Young Sorcerers

Book 1 – Dragon Eggs

by Lisa B. Diamond

1st paperback edition 2013

Library of Congress Cataloging in Publication Data:
Diamond, Lisa S. Brenowitz

The Salem Academy for Young Sorcerers, Book 1: The Dragon Eggs.

1. Rosen, David & Ashira (fictional characters) – fiction. 2. Wizards, witches, and children – fiction. 3. Dragons – fiction. 4. Fantasy. I. Diamond, Lisa S. Brenowitz. II. Young adult series. III. Title.

ISBN-13: 9781484029350

Dedication

This book is dedicated to my son, Joel, who wanted to go to Hogwarts. Thanks to J.K. Rowling for her lovely Harry Potter books. They helped my son find his love of reading.

And, a little bit to Alex – I hope you like it as much as Joel did.

Many thanks to my husband, Richard; my wonderful friends who listened to me tossing ideas around and kept encouraging me, Jennifer G., Caryn A., Catherine E., Nana Andi, and many others. Thanks to Mikey and Joel for helping me with the dragon bits.

Also thanks to Mrs. Crystal Bentley and her lavender crystal from Mountain View Elementary School in Cobb County, Georgia for giving her permission to use her name, her crystal, and her lovely personality in this series.

And, to Smokey, for convincing me to add some personality.

Books by Lisa B. Diamond

For Sale on Amazon in Kindle (ebook) and paperback

The Salem Academy for Young Sorcerers series
The Salem Academy for Young Sorcerers, Book 1: The Dragon Eggs
The Salem Academy for Young Sorcerers, Book 2: The Firebird
The Salem Academy for Young Sorcerers, Book 3: Ancient Runes
The Salem Academy for Young Sorcerers, Book 4: Constellations
The Salem Academy for Young Sorcerers, Book 5: Astronomical Twilight
The Salem Academy for Young Sorcerers, Book 6: Here Be Dragons
The Salem Academy for Young Sorcerers, Book 7: Once Upon A Fairy Tale
The Salem Academy for Young Sorcerers, Book 8: There Be Dragons
The Salem Academy for Young Sorcerers, Book 9: Field Day

Star Light, Faerie Light series
Star Light, Faerie Light
Star Light, Faerie Light, Book 2: The Pixie's Revenge

Table of Contents

Map of the Salem Academy Elementary School Wing

3rd Grade East Classroom	4th Grade East Classroom	5th Grade East Classroom
3rd Grade West Classroom	4th Grade West Classroom	5th Grade West Classroom
Astronomy 1	Elementary School Library	Astronomy 2
Art	Girls Bathroom	Music
Gym	Lunchroom	Stage
	Boys Bathroom	

Prologue

David and his twin sister, Ashira, sat by the pool on an overcast summer afternoon. They were rising third-graders at the local elementary school.

The sky had been threatening to rain for hours, a few drops had even sprinkled down on them, but no thunderstorms had occurred. The lifeguard was on break and everyone else had left the pool due to the light sprinkling of rain.

David's brown hair was cut short in a summer haircut. He loved having a summer haircut as it kept the hair out of his eyes. The shorter his hair was, the happier he was, as long as his head wasn't shaved.

Ashira had long curly red hair pulled back in a ponytail, which she had done herself. She had taken half an hour to decide how she wanted to do her hair before they left for the pool. She had been disappointed no one else was there to see it.

The twins had matching hazel eyes and a small smattering of freckles over their noses. Mrs. Rosen, their mother, sat in the shade watching her children sit at the edge of the pool, waiting for adult swim to be over.

"We're bored," called David to his mother, his blue face mask perched on his forehead.

"Very bored," added Ashira. Her purple goggles were sitting beside her on the ground. She never kept them on for long, but liked to know there were within reach if she needed them.

Ashira reached out and grabbed the beach ball they had brought to the pool and lofted it over her head, before swatting it to her brother.

He didn't move from where he was sitting. Instead, automatically and with no conscious thought in his head, he reached out lazily and plucked it from the air. Without using his hands.

Mrs. Rosen blinked and sat up in her chair abruptly. She noticed the twins' eyes were half-closed, as if they were daydreaming. She saw the ball go back and forth in the air between Ashira and David, without connecting with their hands. Their mother chided herself for not noticing sooner the fragments of magic in the air around the twins, bits swirling almost like tiny droplets clinging to the air.

Mrs. Rosen had been watching and waiting over the last few years to see if anything like this would happen. Not the beach ball itself, but the magical ability. This was the first time she had seen any sign of it. She found it interesting that her children didn't seem to be aware of what they were doing. She quickly placed one hand over the other in the opposite direction, felt the air twitch briefly, and said a few words under her breath, notifying the Salem Academy. She mentally sighed and was glad she had notified the school as magical ability had to be trained.

Mrs. Rosen remembered the first time she had lifted a cookie from the cookie jar, without using her hands. Her mother had scolded her for spoiling her dinner, and Mrs. Rosen had been so surprised that the cookie was actually floating towards her, she had accidentally dropped it into her dog's waiting mouth. She had been five at the time, but the twins had only one magical parent, unlike her, not two.

"Time to go, you two," called Mrs. Rosen to her children.

"Alright," muttered the twins in unison, as they stood up and put their sandals on to walk on the hot summer pavement.

Mrs. Rosen took the beach ball from them and followed them up the path towards the house. As she walked towards the mailbox at the edge of their driveway, she had an idea of what would be inside. She almost knew without looking that there would be two identical letters, one for each of her children, sitting calmly in the plain black metal mailbox. Two letters which their ordinary mail carrier could not possibly have delivered that quickly.

Chapter 1 – The Letters

"Mom? Can I get the mail?" pleaded David, as they walked up the hill towards their house.

"I want to get the mail!" countered Ashira.

Mrs. Rosen settled the argument by getting the mail herself. As she opened the mailbox, she saw the letters.

"Hey! That has my name on it!" said David, looking at the mail in his mother's hands.

"There's one with my name on it, too!" exclaimed Ashira.

"Yes, I know. You may look at it when we get inside after you take your baths," said their mother carefully, knowing full well what the letters said.

"I want to see it now!" said David, trying to grab it out of her hands.

"Wait until we get inside, or you lose all your video game privileges for the rest of the day," replied his mother calmly, knowing he would argue with her and trying to prevent a scene in front of their nonmagical neighbors.

David stood still in his outrage and disbelief. "For the rest of the day?! You can't do that!"

"Can I see mine, Mom?" asked Ashira in a sweet tone. She habitually waited until her twin made their mom mad, and then she would swoop in to get the treat for herself. It usually worked better with their father, though, these days.

"No. But, nice try, sweetie," replied her mother. "Upstairs, both of you."

David read the return address by tilting his head sideways. "What's SAYS? What does that mean?" he asked.

"Inside!" said his mother sternly. She said something under her breath, as the air fluttered around her, and suddenly, David walked to the front door without saying anything else. He took his shower, and dressed immediately into his pajamas. Ashira did the same.

When they came downstairs, Mrs. Rosen sat down in the den and handed the twins their letters. "Go ahead and open them," she encouraged them.

David and Ashira exchanged glances. They had had time to think in their showers about why their mother wouldn't let them have the envelopes, which made them even more curious. They held the envelopes for a moment without opening them and looked at their mother.

"You know what it says, don't you?" asked David quietly.

Mrs. Rosen nodded. She knew what the letters said because she remembered reading her own letter many years ago.

David turned the envelope over in his hand and gave it back to her. "You open it, then."

David didn't like surprises. He wanted to know what something was before he tried it. On the playground, Ashira would be the first to try new equipment. David would follow after her when he knew it was safe, or when he thought someone might make fun of him for his sister doing it first.

David especially didn't like change, and he sensed this letter was about a big change in his young life. The thought of change made him nervous. He stood up and began hopping from foot to foot. His mother tried to convince him to sit down, but he ignored her.

"I can't open the letter. It's addressed to you," his mother replied, not taking the letter.

"So? You opened my birthday cards and read them to me. How is this different?" her son asked.

"It is. Different. Only you can open it. Go ahead. It won't bite," she said with a smile.

He took the letter gingerly and carefully tried to open it. "It won't work!"

Ashira tried to open hers. "Mine won't open either!" She was excited and frustrated. She sensed change, but to her, change was fun.

"Did I give you the wrong ones? Switch them. You can only open the letter addressed to you," explained their mother.

The twins quickly swapped letters. David quickly tore open his to get it over with, while Ashira carefully opened hers in order not to rip it.

David's letter read:

Dear Master David Maxwell Rosen,

Welcome to the Salem Academy for Young Sorcerers! School begins on September 1st. You will be part of the Third Grade East class. Classes will be held during the hours of 9am to 3pm Eastern Standard Time.

The Salem Academy bus will arrive promptly at 8:15am Eastern Standard Time by your mailbox. You will recognize the bus by its burgundy stripe down the center with the Salem Academy logo and mascot on its side.

Open house is on August 15th, from 2-4pm Eastern Standard Time. You will be introduced to your teachers and your classrooms at this time. Parents are encouraged to attend. If you need transportation to Open House, please fill out the attached form, put it in your regular mailbox, and we will be happy to provide it for you. All students will be measured for their school uniforms during Open House.

Don't forget, all visitors must enter the school through the Dragon Foyer, before being allowed to walk back to the Elementary School Wing. Also, no wands or broomsticks will be allowed until ninth grade. ***No exceptions.*** *Any student found in possession of a wand or a broomstick will receive an automatic detention and the wand or broomstick will be confiscated.*

Pets are to be left at home, as they are not allowed at school. Thank you for understanding and keeping the school a cleaner place. Even though the school mascot is a dragon, any student found in possession of a dragon egg, baby dragon, or full grown dragon, will be expelled.

The Third Grade East classroom is in the Elementary School Wing, down the left hallway, last door on the left, overlooking the playground. Attached is a map of the Elementary School Wing for your review.

We look forward to meeting you on August 15th. Please be informed that books will be handed out to students on the first day of class.

Sincerely,

Director Wilhelmina Powers

Chapter 2 – We Can't Do Magic!

Ashira's letter only differed from David's by the name at the top. The twins looked up from their letters.

"What is the Salem Academy?" asked David.

"It's a school of magic," their mother began.

"Why did they send it to us?" interrupted Ashira. "Why would they think..."

"I told them to," said Mrs. Rosen firmly.

"Uh, Mom? Um..." began David. He began hopping from foot to foot again.

"We can't do magic!" continued Ashira. Her fingers nervously pressed the envelope in small folds to create a fan.

Mrs. Rosen picked up the beach ball and floated it above their heads. "Can either of you reach that without using your hands, like you did at the pool today?" The air shimmered as the beach ball hung motionless in the air, almost as if gravity were trying to look the other way.

"We didn't do that at the pool. That's impossible!" declared David. He looked at his mother as if she was crazy.

"Yes, actually, you did. You both did," said their mother in an exasperated tone.

"Mom, what are you talking about?" asked Ashira, absentmindedly picking up crayons and coloring the paper fan she had made out of the folded envelope.

"How are you doing that?" David asked, watching the ball float above his head.

"You will find out on September 1st," she replied, letting the ball drop to the floor. They heard her sigh. "Now I have to find a way to explain this to your father…"

"What do you mean?" asked David. He figured that if getting a letter in the mail didn't surprise his mother, it wouldn't surprise his father. He was wrong.

His mother sighed again. She knew their father would have a difficult time accepting this. He wasn't a wizard himself, and like his son, change made him nervous. Their father had told her when they had children, he didn't want to talk about the possibility of them having magical abilities. He wanted to deal with it if it happened. His reasoning was that they had enough to worry about when their family expanded from two to four people overnight.

"What does this letter mean, Mom?" added Ashira. She almost held her breath in anticipation.

"It means that you and your brother have been accepted to the Salem Academy for Young Sorcerers. It's a good school. I should know. I went there myself," their mother said with a smile.

"You went there!" exclaimed Ashira. "Awesome!"

"What exactly is this school? What does it mean?" asked David suddenly.

"The Salem Academy for Young Sorcerers, or SAYS, is a school which teaches young witches and wizards about how to control their budding magical powers," summarized his mother.

"Does this mean I get a wand?" he asked. In wizarding television shows, the characters always had wands. Wands were cool.

"What did it say in the letter? No wands allowed until high school. No potions until middle school. No broomsticks until high school. No pets, which will be nicer than in my day. Back then, everyone had to bring in a toad, which invariably got squashed, or a rat, which was filthy," she added. "Cats would have been okay if they didn't fight amongst themselves and chase the rats and the toads..."

"No wand?! B-but how do you do magic without a wand?!" objected David.

"Using a wand, in my opinion, is the easy way. It focuses your magical energy for you, without you having to do much. In third through fifth grade, you learn the basics of magic. You learn how to craft spells, gathering the powers around you and focusing the magic. If you haven't crafted your spell correctly, it falls apart," added his mother.

"No wand?!" protested David again.

"Wands have a nasty tendency to backfire when used by beginning wizards and witches, which have caused more problems than I want to remember. No wands!" she said firmly. "Now, go brush your teeth and get ready for bed."

"Where's the school?" Ashira asked.

"I don't really know. It's hidden to keep nonmagical people away. Although, I always suspected it was somewhere in the Midwest, because there's more room out there and less people," said her mother thoughtfully. "I do know it was over an energy vortex, though."

David perked up and left the idea of a wand behind for the moment. "What's an energy vortex?"

"That is place where Earth's energies are more concentrated, such as in spots where there are fault lines from earthquakes, hot springs, or volcanoes. In Georgia, Stone Mountain has an energy vortex rating of five, I believe. I think it's over the Brevard fault line. I know Salem Academy is over a fault line as well. I used to know what it was called. Slanted Creek or something." She paused for a moment, frowning. "Crooked Creek! That's what it was called."

"What kind of uniform?" pressed Ashira, not caring about fault lines. She was more concerned with what she would have to wear to school every day. What if the uniform clashed with her hair?

David didn't care about uniforms. An energy vortex sounded neat, but what about not having a wand or a broomstick?

"You, as a girl, will get a choice of a long skirt or slacks, with a coordinating top. Your brother will get slacks and a shirt. We will find out all about what the uniforms look like during Open House. Don't worry, darling. It won't be too bad. I wore one for ten years and survived. You will, too," said her mother reassuringly.

"No wand? Really?" repeated David disappointingly.

Their mother sighed. The twins knew what the sigh meant. She was going to show them something. Maybe she had a wand...

"Follow me," said their mother tersely.

Chapter 3 – No Wand

The twins followed their mother to her bedroom. They stood in the doorway, watching her dig through one of her drawers.

"You have a wand, don't you!" David said excitedly.

"Actually, no," she replied, turning around to face them. She was holding a small wooden box. She sat down on the floor of her room. The twins sat down next to her, with David on his mother's right side, and Ashira on the left side.

Inside the box were crystals. Different shapes and colors, clear or creamy, pale yellow to deep purple, and every shade in between.

"Pick one," Mrs. Rosen said to her children.

"Can we hold them?" asked Ashira, cautiously.

"That's the only way to tell which one works best for you," Mrs. Rosen smiled.

The twins took turns holding each crystal in the palm of their hands. A pale blue crystal glowed in David's hand. He dropped it in surprise as if it had burned him.

"Are you alright?" asked his mother, as his sister laughed at him.

"Yes. I didn't expect it to glow," David admitted.

Mrs. Rosen looked abashed. "Sorry, honey. I probably should have warned you."

A lavender one glowed in Ashira's hand. After having watched her brother, Ashira knew what to expect. She examined its glow.

"I'll make a necklace for each of you from the crystal you selected and have it ready for you to wear on the first day of school. How does that sound?" asked Mrs. Rosen as she held out her hand for both children to give back their crystals. The twins nodded and grinned.

"Not as good as a wand, but it's cool," Mrs. Rosen heard David say as they left the room.

Later that evening, Ashira sat on her brother's twin bed and stared around the room. David's room was covered in posters of the solar system, planets, a solar eclipse, and any other space paraphernalia he could find. He had always loved space. His ceiling had stars mapped out in a few of the major constellations from the Northern Hemisphere in the sky.

"What do you think about all this?" Ashira asked her brother.

"I don't know. At least we're not in trouble," replied David. He was putting away his legos before bed.

He paused for a moment. "What if they're wrong and we can't do magic?" He knew he could ask Ashira and she wouldn't laugh at him, at least, not about this.

"I don't remember doing it either, but Mom said she saw both of us hit the beach ball at each other without using our hands. I don't think she was imagining it. If she said we did it, then we did," said Ashira loyally. She trusted their mom to guide them in the right direction.

"But a school of magic?" questioned David. "How could it exist?"

"Why couldn't it?" countered his sister. "I wonder what Dad's going to think about all this..."

"What do you mean?" replied David.

"Didn't you hear what Mom said? She went to the Salem Academy. Dad didn't. She doesn't know how she's going to explain all this to him. That means he isn't magical," Ashira observed.

"He could have gone to another school," her twin answered.

"Not if Mom was worried about what he might think," she said firmly.

"Maybe he won't let us go," said David, unsure if he felt happy or sad about it.

"Michelle, why do they have to go to a different school? Why can't they stay at their regular old public school?" Mr. Rosen protested when his wife told him she had registered the twins at the Salem Academy for Young Sorcerers.

"Magical ability must be trained, Philip," Mrs. Rosen said firmly.

"There was one incident. One. Where you thought you saw them perform magic. There's no proof they really are magical. What if you imagined it?" he countered.

Mrs. Rosen raised her eyebrows and then she sighed. She knew she hadn't imagined it. Magic always left traces. "We'll do a test. If I'm right, they go to school at the Salem Academy. If I'm wrong, I will contact the school again and tell them I was wrong. Agreed?"

Mr. Rosen was silent for a minute, then he nodded. "What's the test?"

"I want you to perform the test, that way you will know that I have nothing to do with the children's responses," began Mrs. Rosen.

"How am I supposed to perform a magic test?" demanded Mr. Rosen.

"Simply walk into David's bedroom, and pull all his covers off of him. As for Ashira, try to put covers on top of her. To make it fair, try to put heavy covers on top of her. I will stay in our bedroom, reading a book, with the door closed. I will not know which child's room you enter first, so I have no way of cheating. I trust you to tell me what happens," Mrs. Rosen said with a smile.

Five minutes later, Mr. Rosen walked back into the bedroom he shared with Mrs. Rosen. His mouth was open with an odd expression on his face.

Mrs. Rosen closed her book and laughed. "David pulled his covers back over himself without moving a muscle, didn't he? And, I'm sure Ashira pushed all the covers off of herself without moving as well, didn't she?"

"How did you know?" Mr. Rosen said in astonishment.

"Ashira is hot-natured, and can't stand to have covers on top of her; while David likes as many covers as possible." She paused. "It's like a dam has been lifted, dear. Bits of magic will leak out of the twins, until the floodgates come full force. They must be trained before they hurt someone, or themselves," she said gently, kissing her husband on the cheek.

At breakfast the next morning, David noticed his father kept sticking his spoon back into an empty cereal bowl. "Dad, you already finished your cereal."

Mr. Rosen looked at his bowl for the first time. "Oh, you're right. Thanks, son. Your mother told me about your letter and your sister's. It sounds, um, very interesting."

Mrs. Rosen understood her husband's difficulty in accepting the twins going to a magic school. She said, "Sorry, dear." She kissed her husband on the cheek.

Mr. Rosen blinked several times and put his spoon back into his bowl.

Ashira was re-reading her letter for the umpteenth time.

"Mom, what's Third Grade East mean?" asked David. He turned and frowned at his sister. That was her question, not his. He wanted to know the answer, too, but he hated that she made him ask for her. She had a habit of getting her brother to ask hard questions for her.

Ashira sat down at the kitchen table and looked at her mother expectantly.

"SAYS is the sorcerers' school for North America, which includes the United States of America and southern Canada. If I remember correctly, Third Grade East includes all the students from the Newfoundland, Atlantic, Eastern, and

Central time zones. That's why your school hours are from nine in the morning until three in the afternoon. The Newfoundland time zone children will be attending from ten-thirty to four-thirty. The Atlantic time zone children will be attending from ten to four, and Central will attend from eight to two. Which means all four time zones will be able to be in one set of classes.

"Third Grade West includes Mountain, Pacific, Alaska, and Hawaii. Their times are staggered as well to accommodate four different time zones. There aren't enough children to split up the third grade with less time zones, unfortunately. I think Hawaii starts at 7:30 in the morning, with Mountain time starting as late as 10:30 for all of Third Grade West to be together," she continued.

"Although," added their mother, "there is a small magical school somewhere around the border of Northern Canada and Alaska, which is also available for students coming from Hawaii. If I remember correctly, it's primarily geared towards the First Nation tribe students. Different cultures have different approaches to magic. If a student is accepted to one magical school, she or he can petition to go to a different one if the time zone or learning style would be more favorable."

"What do we learn there?" asked Ashira, feeling comfortable enough with the topic to ask her own question. Change was fun to rush into, but when she slowed down enough to look around, sometimes she was as nervous as David.

Chapter 4 – What Do We Learn There?

"Astronomy…" began Mrs. Rosen. She was interrupted by a delighted yell from her son. She grinned and continued. "Basic spell construction, animal and plant natures, the history of magic in America. You know, the basics. In third grade, you're getting acclimated to magic."

A buzzer sounded.

It was a reminder that Mr. Rosen had to leave now in time to catch his bus to work. Mrs. Rosen sighed and put her hands together for a moment as the air rippled around her. She had promised her husband the previous evening that if he appeared upset, she would temporarily help him to forget his distress and focus on work. Suddenly, Mr. Rosen stood up, kissed his wife and daughter on their cheeks, patted his son on the back, and walked out the door.

"Mom, you didn't!" exclaimed Ashira. She noticed how her father went from being upset to calm in a few seconds.

She felt her mom must have put a spell on her dad, and she didn't feel that was right.

"What didn't she do?" asked David. He looked up in surprise at Ashira's tone of voice.

"She put a spell on him. Didn't you, Mom?" said Ashira.

"Put a spell on who?" asked David, now thoroughly confused.

"Your father is having a bit of a hard time adjusting to the news of there being a new wizard and witch in the family. I merely encouraged him to forget about it for a few hours so he could concentrate on work," admitted their mother.

"Did you make Daddy fall in love with you?" asked Ashira.

"No! Of course, not!" Mrs. Rosen sighed. "Actually, it was because of your father that I changed my career. You see, I was offered a teaching position at the Brazilian magic school and turned it down to stay here in Georgia and be with your father."

"All these years he hasn't known that you're magical?" asked David.

"People believe what they choose to believe, son," said his mother enigmatically, as she cleared away the breakfast dishes.

"What do you mean?" David asked. "He didn't know you were a witch?"

"He has always known that I have abilities which are different from his own. He normally chooses not to question me about them, as what your father doesn't completely understand, makes him a little nervous," their mother admitted. "Shoes on, children. We have to go to the grocery store."

"Mom?" began David. "How do we get there?"

"Get where?" replied his mother. They were at the grocery store. Ashira was picking out apples, while David was staring at the strawberries.

"Um, our new school," he said in a whisper.

"Oh," smiled Mrs. Rosen. "You can call it the Salem Academy in public. It's registered as a private school in order that we don't receive a call from the truancy officers."

"What's a truancy officer?" asked Ashira.

"People in the state government responsible for making sure you and your brother are enrolled in some sort of accepted school program from first grade through twelfth, or until you receive your high school diploma," explained their mother.

"What about kindergarten?" David said.

"Kindergarten is voluntary in the state of Georgia at this time," said Mrs. Rosen. "Oh, and a bus will take you to school every morning."

"No, I mean, how do we get there for Open House?" asked David. He was intrigued by the idea of a magical school bus. He wondered what else it could do.

"Ah, yes. Well, I can take us there. All of us. But, I think it would make your father rather uncomfortable. So, we're taking the Salem Academy bus. It will help ease your father's fears, and at the same time, get you accustomed to taking the correct bus in the morning," said his mother.

"Will there be more than one bus?" asked David.

His mother shook her head. "I believe it's picking us up at 1:15pm, which will give us a chance to walk around the school grounds before Open House begins."

Chapter 5 – Waiting for the Bus

The morning of August fifteenth dawned bright and early. The twins took turns watching the clock all morning until lunchtime. They quickly ate their lunch of peanut butter and jam with apple slices on the side and a yogurt drink before glancing at the clock again. Their father was working from home in the morning in order to take the afternoon off to go with them to Open House.

"What does the building look like?" asked Ashira. She wore a lavender dress with pretty white sandals, and a white bow in her hair. She kept fidgeting with her bow.

"Does it look like a castle?" asked David eagerly. He always associated magic with wizards and stone castles and magic wands.

His mother had convinced him to wear shorts and a nice short-sleeved shirt. He was walking from window to window in the downstairs to try and get the first glimpse of the bus.

"A castle? In the United States?" his mother smiled and ruffled his hair. "The Salem Academy looks like a normal private school building. There are three wings. One for the Elementary School, for third through fifth grades; one for the Middle School, for sixth through eighth grades; and, one for the High School, for ninth through twelfth grades. The smallest one is the Elementary School, and the largest one is the High School," added their mother.

"That makes sense," said their father.

"Although, the school is made from more durable materials than a normal school building," their mother continued thoughtfully. "As it wouldn't be good for anything to catch on fire while you are learning the basics of magic, would it?"

Their father groaned and sighed audibly. The twins exchanged glances.

"That is one of the reasons why I didn't want to teach you at home. The main reason, of course, is that the Salem Academy is a good school," said their mother.

"Better than the Brazilian school you were going to teach at?" their father asked, nonchalantly.

"Well, I tend to be a little biased as I went their myself," Mrs. Rosen admitted. "But, I do think so, yes. Although, the Brazilian school is a lovely one as well."

As the family was walking out their front door, Ashira suddenly looked up at her mother. "Are we supposed to bring anything?"

"No," said David, glancing at his mother. "If we were, Mom would have packed it in a backpack or bag, or something."

Their mother nodded in agreement and smiled.

"Is the mascot really a dragon?" whispered David.

"Yes," smiled his mother. "If I remember correctly, it's a white dragon for Elementary School, a heather gray dragon for Middle School, and a dark red dragon for High School."

"Cool!" David said.

"It's a dragon sitting on a crystal ball," added their mother.

"You mean like the one on top of your dresser?" asked Ashira. She always noticed little details that her brother missed.

"Yes. Exactly like that," their mother admitted.

"I always wondered why you had a dragon on your dresser," commented David. "Are there any dragons at school?"

"Of course there aren't!" said Ashira. "Didn't you read your letter? It said no dragons allowed at school."

David made a face at his sister. He felt that she was showing off again. "Mom, are there really no dragons at school?" Dragons were cool. Cooler than wands, even.

"No dragons, honey. It's too dangerous for the students, as well as the dragons. Sorry, love," she replied. She looked at his crestfallen face. "Don't worry. When you're in high school, they'll take you on a field trip to see dragons."

"We have to wait until high school?!" groaned David. "Why would it be dangerous?"

Mr. Rosen had an answer for this one, "Because they breathe fire! Although, I admit, the thought of dragons is fascinating. But, I wouldn't want you children to get hurt!"

"Well, honey, not all of them breathe fire, but you are right, dragons can be quite dangerous. You see, children, there used to be a dragon colony not too far from the school. Some of the high schoolers would dare each other to sneak into the colony and try to steal the eggs. First, that was unfair to the dragons. The eggs didn't get a chance to grow and mature to be able to hatch into baby dragons. Second, many of the students stupid enough to try this would get hurt or killed by the mother dragons protecting their eggs," finished Mrs. Rosen.

"There really are dragons?" Mr. Rosen questioned. He had always loved dragons.

"Yes, dear," Mrs. Rosen answered.

Real dragons, thought Mr. Rosen. *Maybe this magic stuff wasn't so bad after all. As long as the dragons kept their claws and their fiery breath away from his children, that was.*

Chapter 6 – The Bus Ride

As the Salem Academy bus pulled up to their mailbox, Mr. Rosen said, "How is a normal bus going to take us there?"

For the Salem Academy bus looked like a normal yellow-orange school bus with a broad maroon stripe running across the middle of the bus. It had the words "The Salem Academy" in small letters above the stripe and in the back of the bus.

Mrs. Rosen smiled. "Where did you get the idea it was a normal bus?"

The four of them climbed aboard the bus.

David said, "Cool!" as he hurried to grab a seat.

The seats were set up with plush burgundy benches seating two to three people on each side of a table. Each seat had a seatbelt. The windows were tinted and did not open, although other than that, they seemed to be normal bus windows, and they displayed the outside world as any normal window would.

Mr. Rosen sat next to David with a slightly stunned look on his face. "Comfortable seat," he grunted.

Mrs. Rosen was bemused as she sat down opposite her son.

"Fasten your seat belts, children," Mrs. Rosen gently admonished.

The door to the bus closed with a *whoosh*! A few moments later, the bus stopped again at a completely different mailbox.

"Mom, why is there a pink house and palm trees?" asked David.

"Looks like Florida to me," replied his mother matter-of-factly.

"Florida?" said their father disbelievingly. He gave a quick glance around and decided he would close his eyes for the rest of the trip, as he did every morning on the bus ride to work. Maybe a little nap would be refreshing. He leaned back against the plush burgundy seat.

"Yes, dear," replied Mrs. Rosen, patting her husband's hand, and winking at the twins.

A boy with longish blond hair climbed on the bus. He had the attitude and clothing of someone who was used to living by the beach. All tanned skin and white teeth, with a forced relaxed stride. He was followed closely by his mother, who had the air of one wanting her son to desperately have manners and not embarrass her. He saw David and Ashira, and nodded. He turned to David and said, "Dude, word."

"Huh?" replied David.

"Eric, introduce yourself properly," snapped his mother.

"Name's Eric Knieling from Daytona Beach," said the beach boy morosely.

David and Ashira introduced themselves as the bus closed its door again.

A few moments later, they were by another mailbox. David noticed a cream stucco house and more palm trees. "Are we still in Florida?" he asked.

Their mother shook her head. "Florida has white, white sands on its beaches. We're further north. One of the Carolinas, by the look of it."

Another boy climbed on the bus. He had black hair and bright blue eyes, and his favorite color was obviously green, as that was the color of his backpack and his clothes. His clothes were neat and tidy, he walked with quiet assurance, as if he felt he belonged on a bus going to a magic school. He was followed by his mother and his father.

He immediately introduced himself as Sean Shaughnessy from Charleston, South Carolina. David and Ashira thought he seemed nice. His family sat in the seats behind the Rosens. Suddenly, Mrs. Rosen said, "Colleen? Is that you?" to Sean's mother.

"Michelle? As I live and breathe!" replied Mrs. Shaughnessy. The two mothers hugged and sat down again.

"Sean's mother and I were in class together at the Salem Academy. We were among the only redheads there, weren't we?" grinned Mrs. Rosen.

Mrs. Shaughnessy smiled and nodded. The two mothers chatted while the two fathers introduced themselves.

"Is your father magical, too?" asked David.

Sean nodded. "Magic has always been in our house. Are both your parents magical?"

The twins shook their heads. "When we received our letters, Mom had to tell Dad about it," began David.

"He wasn't sure if he wanted us to go to the Salem Academy," added Ashira.

Eric's contribution to their conversation was to mutter the word, "Dude" a few more times and nod.

Several more students came on the bus with their parents. They were fourth or fifth graders. David and Ashira were fascinated to see all the places the bus stopped.

"Am I the only third grade girl?" Ashira whispered to David. He shrugged.

"Honey, not all the children in your class will be riding the bus," Mrs. Rosen reminded her daughter.

When a giggling girl with dark curly hair named Lily climbed aboard the bus, Ashira gave a sigh of relief. Her mother climbed aboard after her, announcing loudly, "I thought you said this was a normal school bus." The girl giggled more.

Ashira introduced herself and nudged her brother to do so as well.

Chapter 7 – About the Bus

Another girl climbed aboard at the next stop. She seemed sweet-natured and well-mannered. She was wearing a pretty pink dress, which matched her personality. She took one look at Ashira's hair and told her she looked like Anne of Green Gables.

"Who's that?" asked David.

"*Anne of Green Gables* is the first book in a series by Lucy Maud Montgomery. The main character, Anne, has red hair," explained his sister, loftily.

The girl introduced herself as Rebecca Montgomery, Lucy Maud Montgomery's very distant descendant, from Prince Edward Island.

Twin Vietnamese boys climbed aboard next. They were from Halifax, Nova Scotia. One was a practical joker, and the other was quiet, unsure of what to do next.

An African-American girl from New Orleans with pretty long black braids, climbed aboard. She had to cajole her mother into getting on the bus. She had a lovely Cajun accent.

More fourth and fifth graders climbed aboard.

"Where are they going?" asked David, watching as the students disappeared down the aisle.

"Second floor," replied his mother.

"But there is no second floor..." said David.

"Isn't there?" said his mother with a twinkle in her eyes. "Oh, and you aren't allowed to get up while the bus is moving."

David and Ashira looked at each other, and then back at their mother.

"How many floors are there?" asked Ashira.

"As many as needed," her mother replied.

"Really?" David asked, his eyes wide. "Are they all like this one?"

"Yes," answered Sean. "Only they disappear when the bus empties out, so you have to be one of the last ones on the bus in order to climb to the upper floors."

"Have you ever climbed higher than the first level?" David asked.

"No, this is my first time on the bus. My mom told me about it, though," Sean sighed. "I'd like to try it after school starts, maybe on the way home. But you have to time it just right. If you arrive too late, my mom says the bus leaves without you and you have to ride with the middle schoolers. She says they aren't nice to the elementary school kids."

"No, they aren't," Mrs. Rosen agreed.

"Are there going to be more kids in the Third Grade East class?" asked David.

"Oh, yes, definitely," said Mrs. Shaughnessy with a smile. "Keep in mind, not everyone is on the bus today," she said, repeating what Mrs. Rosen had already told Ashira.

"There are still children who have not received their letters yet," added Mrs. Rosen.

"Really? They haven't received their letters? Why not?" David asked.

"Late bloomers," Mrs. Shaughnessy replied. "Some don't receive their letters until right before school starts, in another month."

David looked confused.

"Some children don't show their magical talent until they are triggered in some way, such as starting a new school year, getting surprised by something, or even going through puberty," Mrs. Rosen explained. "All the hormones seem to trigger their magical ability, if they have any. Not all children of magical parents are magical themselves."

"Why not?" asked Ashira.

"Why do you have red hair and not your brother, sweetie?" countered Mrs. Rosen. "Traits carried in our DNA.

The same reason why you and your brother can curl your tongue, and I cannot."

"Are there any more stops?" asked David.

"Are we there yet?" asked Sean.

Mrs. Shaughnessy rolled her eyes. "Has the bus stopped in front of a large school building? If not, then we are still picking up children."

"We're here!" squealed Ashira, pointing to a large school building.

Chapter 8 – The Dragon Foyer

The Salem Academy was built out of white marble and heather gray swirled granite. It looked like a typical private school that had somehow landed in the middle of nowhere.

"Wow! It's beautiful!" said Ashira in awe. Her eyes were shining. She looked at her twin brother, trying to figure out his reaction.

David stared at the school behind the iron gates. He could see the main Dragon Foyer building ahead of them. It looked as if the Elementary School Wing was on the far left, because he caught a glimpse of what looked to be playground equipment. He saw a running track made of soft red clay on the far right, next to what must be the High School Wing.

David felt frustrated by the fact there were no real live dragons at the school. After all, the mascot was a dragon! He understood that his mom had told him dragons weren't safe, but still, this was a magic school! He turned to Sean. "No dragons, huh?"

Sean nodded. "Yeah, a bummer isn't it."

Ashira rolled her eyes. "Boys!" she muttered. All the amazing possibilities of being at a magic school, and they had to focus on the one of the few things that wasn't there. How ridiculous!

Her mother took her hand as they walked through the front doors of the school, which were open wide for Open House, and into the Dragon Foyer. On the inside of the school, the air danced with the magic which flowed through the school. It was almost tangible. Even Mr. Rosen noticed the difference, as he turned his head to look around, trying to figure out what it was.

There was a beautiful water color painting of a white dragon on the left wall. It looked as if it was giggling. A lovely painting of a deep heather gray dragon done in acrylics resided on the back wall. The look on its face was more serious. A handsome oil painting of a dark red dragon was on the right wall. The dragon in it looked downright cranky. In the middle of the room was a large black granite desk with swirls of white stars running through it. Behind the desk sat three women with name tags.

Mrs. Opal Palmistry was a dark-haired, olive-skinned Semitic looking woman who was short with a large nose. Mrs. Crystal Ball was a large, round, sweet-natured African-American woman. Mrs. Tara Cards was a dark-haired, thin, flat animated Korean-American woman who seemed to be always talking.

"New students!" shrieked Mrs. Cards in delight. "Oh, goody, goody. You will all be needing new uniforms! How exciting. Where are the tape measures, Crystal?"

"Calm down, Tara, calm down. You'll scare them!" Mrs. Ball said before turning to the new students. "Remember, we have to measure everyone. I'm sure they've all grown over the summer. Let's see, we have three tape measures..." she said trailing off. She took the tape measures and put them on the counter. Then she snapped her fingers and the space behind each tape measure had magically become roped off to form a line.

"All returning students, please enter the first line on the right. All new students, please enter the last two lines on the left. Thank you for your cooperation, children," called out Mrs. Ball.

Sean picked up one of the tape measures and held it up. "What are we supposed to do with it?"

A fourth grader snorted at him in the next line over, muttering, "Newbie!" and stood calmly as the tape measure moved over the length of the student's arms and legs measuring.

David and Sean stared with open mouths watching the tape measure finish measuring the student and then tap a number on the counter. Mrs. Palmistry pulled out several pairs of pants and several shirts from a large box and gave them to the student. "Next," she said.

Mrs. Ball took the tape measure out of his hands gently, and said kindly, "Honey, let me do that." As the tape measure evaluated Sean, David watched with his mouth still open.

"You're going to catch flies with that, if you don't shut it soon," said Mrs. Ball nicely. She let the tape measure evaluate David, as she pulled out pants and shirts from another large box for Sean. The pants were heather gray, the shirts were white with a little white dragon on top of an embroidered circle of burgundy. They also had jackets, scarves, hats, gloves, sweaters, and knit vests.

"What are the girls' choices?" asked David. He whirled around to stare at his sister. "Why did you make me say that?!" he snarled. He hated when his sister prodded him mentally to say something instead of saying it herself. It was a habit he was hoping she would grow out of soon.

Ashira merely smiled at her brother and stepped forward.

Chapter 9 – Measurements

"You couldn't get to the front fast enough, could you, dear?" asked Mrs. Ball kindly. "Well, sweetie, the only difference between the girls' choices and the boys' choices would be the fact that you can also have a long heather gray pleated skirt, if you want. We tried to do a gray and burgundy plaid pleated skirt, but somehow, the dark reds never seem to match from the skirt to the tops, so we stopped that."

Mrs. Ball paused and lowered her voice. "Personally, I think someone who didn't like plaid hexed the uniforms." She raised her voice again and snapped her fingers, as the tape measure took Ashira's measurements as well.

Then she handed Sean, David, and Ashira their uniforms with a smile and a wave. The three of them started to walk away, when David paused.

"Um, Mrs. Ball, what do we do next?" asked David, nervously. He somehow felt that he could trust Mrs. Ball to steer him in the right direction.

"I suggest you follow your mother to your classroom. She looks like she knows the way there. That is, of course, assuming that the woman on the other side of the room is your mother, and she looks exactly like your sister standing next to you," said Mrs. Ball.

"How did you know she was my sister?" asked David, surprised.

"This is your first time here, dear. Who else would make you say something you didn't want to other than your family?" replied Mrs. Ball shrewdly, referring to how Ashira had made David ask about the girls' choices for the uniforms.

David, Sean, and Ashira walked over to where their parents were standing by the portrait of the white dragon.

"Your teachers aren't quite ready for you, yet. So, we've decided to walk around the campus," said Mrs. Rosen.

"What do we do with all these clothes?" asked David, not wanting to carry a large bundle of clothes everywhere.

"Oh, right. Sorry, love," said Mrs. Rosen. She placed one of her hands on top of the other one in the opposite direction, murmured something indistinctly, and instantly the bags of clothes David and Ashira had been holding disappeared.

"Where did they go?" asked David, looking shocked. All this magic stuff took a bit of getting used to.

"She sent them home, silly," replied Ashira confidently, holding out her hand to her mother.

Mrs. Rosen took her daughter's hand, and the seven of them walked back outside.

David noticed that Sean's mother had sent his clothes home as well.

"We're going to show you the outside first," said Mrs. Shaughnessy.

They didn't get very far. The children saw the playground equipment and ran to play. The parents stood and chatted by the sidelines.

On top of one of the pieces of playground equipment was a mini telescope. David was looking through it around the property.

"Mom? What is that fence for?" called out David, referring to the huge wrought iron fence several feet in front of them.

"It surrounds the property so that no one can get in," answered Sean. He turned and pointed, "Up there, my mom told me is the astronomy tower. Only, we don't get to use it for some reason."

Chapter 10 – About the School

"That doesn't make sense," David declared. "If we're studying astronomy, why wouldn't we get to use the astronomy tower?"

"Time zones," called out Ashira, waving a piece of paper. "This is a brochure for the school. Third through Fifth Grades West use the astronomy tower here. Third through Fifth Grades East use an astronomy tower on Prince Edward Island. They want us to be as far east in the time zones as possible so we can study the night sky earlier in the evening. They don't want us to stay up until midnight."

"Didn't we meet someone from Prince Edward Island?" asked Sean.

"Yes. Rebecca Montgomery. The pale girl with dark hair. She seemed really sweet," Ashira replied. She looked thoughtful for a moment, as if considering something carefully. "You know, I actually kind of like the uniforms."

"I thought you'd complain because they were red," said her twin.

Ashira looked surprised that her brother had noticed.

"What? Grandma gave you that red dress for your birthday and you had a fit!" said David.

"That was bright red. Bright orange red clashes with my hair. Maroon is a blue red and actually looks good with my hair," said Ashira in a dignified tone, repeating something her mother had told her.

"You are such a girl," said her brother.

Ashira stuck her tongue out at her brother and said, "Yes, I am. I still think I like the uniforms."

"Yeah, they're okay. I wish they had more blue in them," added David, as blue was his favorite color.

"I wish they had more green in them," Sean said, as green was his favorite color. "Oh, well. My mom said that's what weekends are for."

"Huh?" asked David, confused.

"Wearing other colors," pointed out Sean. He seemed more comfortable in the surroundings. Magic didn't seem to surprise him, as it did David.

"Oh, yeah..." David said. "At least they're not button-down shirts and ties."

"That would never have worked," said Ashira matter-of-factly. "You still can't tuck in your shirt!" She liked to have her clothes neat, orderly, and coordinating, like her hair accessories.

"I don't see why I should have to," muttered David mutinously. He liked to pick the first shirt in his drawer to wear and grab a pair of soccer shorts to match. Most of his soccer shorts were black, and he never noticed the ones which weren't.

"You don't have to," Sean said. "They're polo shirts. I'm glad we don't have ties. I hate ties. Hey, I like our mascot."

"The dragon?" said David. "Yeah. That's pretty cool."

"I think it's cute," said Ashira.

"Cute?" her twin said in an outraged tone. "Dragons aren't cute. They breathe fire. They're fierce."

Ashira raised her eyebrows and said, "I still think it's cute. Not cuddly, but cute. Besides, not all dragons breathe fire. Mom said so."

"Whatever! Girls!" muttered her brother.

"It says here that no one can arrive magically inside the gate," continued Ashira, reading the pamphlet on the school.

"What does that mean?" asked David.

"No transportation spells," Sean told them.

"What's a transportation spell?" David asked.

"You know, a spell which moves you from one place to another," Sean said.

"How could they stop you?" asked David.

"Enchantments," said Sean. "Powerful enchantments."

"What else does the brochure say, Ashira?" asked her brother, curiously.

"Well, it tells about the history of the school. The school began in Salem, Massachusetts in 1703 after the witch burnings, to teach real witches and wizards how to avoid being burned at the stake or drowned in water. The school continued in Salem until 1903, when it was combined with one from California, and moved out here," said Ashira.

"Where is here?" asked Sean.

"Our mom thought it was in the Midwest," replied David. He was surprised Sean didn't know where the school was either. "She said there was more room and less people than the Northeast."

"Time to go inside, kids," yelled Mr. Rosen, pointing to his watch.

David, Sean, and Ashira all looked at each other, wondering what the classrooms would be like.

Chapter 11 – The Elementary School Wing

David, Ashira, and Sean walked back to the Dragon Foyer.

"Where do we go?" asked David, looking around.

"Honey," began Mrs. Ball. "You're in the Elementary School Wing. Go through the white dragon," she gestured.

"Through?" Sean said in disbelief. He hadn't walked through anything before now.

"Through," Mrs. Shaughnessy stated, as she walked through the picture. Mr. Shaughnessy followed his wife with a wink to the children. Sean followed his father, and then poked his head back into the Dragon Foyer.

"Come on, David. Come on, Ashira," Sean said encouragingly, his head seemingly floating in mid-air.

David blinked hard and walked through the picture.

Ashira glanced back at her mother, who nodded, and followed her brother. Mrs. Rosen grabbed her husband's hand, and pulled him after the twins.

Ashira bumped into David as he stood there, in a long hallway, staring at Sean's back. He wasn't sure if he wanted to go forward or stay where he was.

"What are you doing?" demanded Ashira, trying to figure out why her brother wasn't walking forward. She was excited to meet their new teachers.

"Which way do we go?" David asked the air.

"We probably want to follow the signs," pointed out Ashira. She was the observant one, who liked details. Her brother was good at following through once he found his path.

The hallway ahead of them branched into two directions. To the left, the signs announced third and fourth grade. To the right, the signs announced fourth and fifth grade.

"How is that possible?" David asked, reading the signs.

"Well, if third grade is on the left and fifth is on the right, that must mean that fourth is in the middle," reasoned his sister.

Sean stepped back to join them. "She's also holding the map of the school," he added. Sean seemed confident as he walked through the hallway, while David was still in awe of the fact they were in a school of magic.

The third grade classrooms were at the end of the hall. Third Grade East was the last classroom on the left, overlooking the playground. There were about a dozen other boys and girls in the classroom already. They recognized some of them from the bus ride.

Rebecca and Lily walked over to join Ashira. The three girls stood chatting about the school uniforms, and whether they preferred the idea of wearing skirts or pants. None of them had ever been in private school before with uniforms, and the idea of uniforms was odd to them.

David and Sean were joined by the twins from Halifax, Noah and Zachary. The boys were discussing how amazing it would be to see a real dragon. They debated which color dragon would be the coolest to see.

Two boys walked up to join them. They introduced themselves as Michael and Parker. They were both very sure of themselves and couldn't wait to tell the other boys that they knew all the answers to whatever anyone else was discussing.

David and Sean exchanged a knowing glance. They had both met show-offs before.

An African-American boy named Jacob walked up to Zachary Sawyer, pulled a quarter out of his ear, and handed it to him. Zachary started laughing, reached over to Jacob's ear, pulled the selfsame quarter out, and handed it back to Jacob.

The two boys walked away from the group, discussing magic tricks. Eric joined them.

Noah, Zachary's twin, sighed. "I hate that trick! Now, he's going to be doing that the whole way home!"

"I understand. I hate it when my twin focuses on something and I have to listen to it for days on end," sympathized David.

"Yeah, but people don't expect you to be like your sister because she's a girl. They expect Zach and me to be alike because we're both boys," grumbled Noah.

There was a loud giggle heard from the girls standing nearby. Lily was giggling at Jacob pulling a quarter out of her ear. Rebecca shook her head at Jacob and backed away. Unfortunately, she inadvertently backed up into Rachel from New York City.

"Hey, you, watch where you're going!" said Rachel.

"Sorry!" murmured Rebecca, looking embarrassed.

Chapter 12 – Students, Students, Everywhere

"She didn't mean to bump into you," exclaimed Ashira, jumping to Rebecca's defense. Lily agreed.

"I'm Hailey. I'm from New Orleans. What's your name?" said the African-American girl with a pronounced Southern drawl. She was obviously trying to divert the other girl's attention. Rebecca looked relieved.

"I'm Rachel. I'm from New York City," replied the Chinese-American girl in a clipped New York accent.

"Children, children, quiet down," called a voice from the front of the classroom.

The children hushed immediately and turned to look at their new teacher. Mrs. Dray had short dark straight hair which framed her head and burgundy rimmed glasses. Her clothes were neat, but not overly so. She looked friendly, but firm, and quite organized.

David thought she looked surprisingly normal. He had somehow expected her to wear a witch's hat and cape, instead of a standard school uniform dress.

Ashira noticed the teacher wore a crystal necklace and had a pair of glasses on her desk.

"My name is Mrs. Dray, and I am the teacher for the Third Grade East class of the Salem Academy. Third Grade West is next door, and the Fourth Grade classes are across the hall." As she said this, a handful of students looked embarrassed and left the room, presumably to the Third Grade West classroom next door.

"I have laid out all of your school books on the table under the window for your perusal, if you wish. There is also a stack of papers next to the books. This stack contains your syllabus and your weekly schedule. Before you take a weekly schedule, please make sure you have the correct time zone to avoid any confusion. Feel free to ask me any questions and thank you for coming."

"Psst, Ashira, what does 'perusal' mean?" David whispered to his sister.

"It means we can look at the books if we want to," she whispered back to him. They both wandered over to the table, along with the rest of the students to see their new schoolbooks.

There were five basic textbooks:

1. Stars and How to Calculate Where to Find Them by Etoile Estimates for Astronomy
2. Basic Spell Construction for Third Graders by Diana Wicca
3. The Nature of Plants by Herb Botany
4. Exploring Animals and Their Habitats by Harry Zoo
5. The History of Magic in America by Tituba and Elizabeth Parris

David was leafing through the Astronomy textbook happily, only pausing to show some of the text to Sean, or whoever else would pay attention. Sean liked stars, but his first love was music.

Ashira was looking at their weekly schedule. She liked how orderly it was. She walked up to her mother, who was speaking with Mrs. Dray. Normally, Ashira was hesitant about asking questions of people she didn't know, but she felt it was okay as her mother was standing there. "Why do we have late days on Wednesdays?"

"You interrupted, Ashira. Remember your manners," reminded her mother.

"Sorry. My name is Ashira. It's nice to meet you, Mrs. Dray," began Ashira. When Mrs. Dray nodded, Ashira continued, "Why do we have late days on Wednesdays?"

Mrs. Dray smiled. "You only have late days on Wednesdays from November 1st through March 1st, due to your Astronomy practicals. Which means that you will get to study the night sky during those months. Third Grade East uses the observatory on Prince Edward Island."

Chapter 13 – Astronomy

"How neat!" exclaimed Ashira. "Maybe Rebecca will show us around." She glanced around the room to look for Rebecca, whom she considered a new friend.

"Do you have any other questions for Mrs. Dray?" Mrs. Rosen asked her daughter.

"What if we really can't do magic?" whispered Ashira.

"Then you wouldn't have received the letter," Mrs. Dray responded confidently.

"Really?" Ashira said.

"Really," replied Mrs. Dray, confidently. She stood next to Ashira and gave her a little hug and said, "I get that question every year in Open House from at least five different students."

"Thank you, Mrs. Dray," Ashira said, beaming.

"Not at all, not at all. I look forward to seeing you on September 1st," said Mrs. Dray cheerily.

"Go get your brother and tell him we're going to meet the Astronomy teacher, Mrs. Celestra," Mrs. Rosen told her daughter. "Tell him she has crystals that glow like stars and cover the ceiling."

The Astronomy room really did have crystals that glowed like stars which covered the ceiling. They were tiny crystals of varying colors placed to show the night sky in the Northern Hemisphere.

Mr. Rosen loved astronomy almost as much as David did. He exclaimed over the crystals on the ceiling, urging David to try to find Orion, which was David's favorite constellation.

Mrs. Celestra looked exactly as Ashira thought an Astronomy teacher, who was a witch, should look. She had shoulder-length brown hair with blond streaks, which was bushy and wavy. She wore sparkly glasses and the dragon on the Salem Academy logo on her dress even seemed to shine like a star from the night sky.

Mrs. Celestra pressed a button to slowly turn the sky to reflect how the sky changed during the year, including adding Venus and Mars when they were present in the sky. She pressed another button to display the night sky in the Southern Hemisphere. All of the students who had wandered into the room, oohed and ahhed to see it.

Both of the twins liked her as she shimmered with positive energy.

Mrs. Celestra was impressed with how many of the constellations David knew.

"You know what that means, of course," replied Mrs. Celestra, her eyes twinkling, after David had pointed out most of the constellations overhead. "I shall have to give you a few extra special research assignments while everyone else is learning their star charts."

"That would be awesome!" David responded enthusiastically.

After they had thanked Mrs. Celestra for her time and said how much the twins would look forward to the first day of school in her class, they moved onto the Art classroom. Their art teacher, Mr. Warhol, had displayed at a table against the window of how different things in nature, such as herbs, spices, tree bark, plants, and invertebrates make colors.

He obviously liked repetition, as he had drawn one picture four times, each time using a different mixture of herbs, or other bits from nature, to make the colors he used.

The twins thought him a little odd. Even his appearance was dramatic, for he was tall and thin with untidy white hair, bright blue eyes, and thick dark-rimmed glasses. His clothes had smears of the herbs, as if he had used his clothes to wipe off his hands.

The classroom itself was almost like a big easel, with paper everywhere, waiting to be used. Ashira was the artist,

David only painted when there was nothing else to do. But, even David had to admit that this new way of working with herbs and other odd bits from nature to make colors was interesting, as it seemed more like a science experiment than coloring a silly book.

Mrs. Rosen pointed out different colors for Mr. Rosen. He reviewed them dutifully, fascinated in spite of himself to see the variety of different shades from natural sources, and knew his daughter must love this room.

The walls of the music room were covered with pictures of instruments and music. Their teacher, Mr. Amadeus, was short and stout, with light brown hair, dark blue eyes, and a large nose. He had a frown on his face and he looked quite unpleasant.

"Music is everything," he announced in a booming voice, as David, Sean, and Ashira walked into his room. "This year, we will cultivate your voices. Next year, you will choose an instrument." He winked at them and said, "Only kidding.

We're going to make a few hand instruments this year. Come and let me show you a few ways to hear Earth's sounds."

Ashira and David exchanged a confused glance. Sean looked joyful. His dad had helped conduct a sunset once.

Mrs. Rosen smiled. "I loved this class! I always found it hard to pick a favorite sound." She picked up one of the wooden sticks leaning against the far wall, and turned it upside down. The effect was like hearing a mini rainstorm, which was somehow soothing to the children, as the different surprises over the course of the afternoon, from teacher to teacher, had been somewhat unsettling for them.

Mr. Rosen, who loved music, liked the rainstorm effect. He paid close attention to what Mr. Amadeus had to say.

Mr. Amadeus said, "That, my children, is called a rainstick." He waved his hands in the direction of the opposite corner of the room. "Those are called hand drums, otherwise known as tambourines. You will learn how to make them this year."

"Cool!" said David and Sean at the same time.

"Can any of you tell me a few other sounds of nature?" Mr. Amadeus asked them.

"The ocean?" answered Ashira instantly. She loved the beach, as did her brother.

"The wind," Sean replied, remembering hearing the wind whistle through the trees near his house.

"Good job, children. You are both right. As Mr. Warhol teaches you how to paint a picture using colors made from nature, I will be teaching you how to create a scene, a picture, with sounds from nature. Close your eyes for a moment and listen," Mr. Amadeus said.

The children closed their eyes and heard the sound of waves crashing to shore, seagulls flying overhead, and a gentle wind rustling through the tall palm trees.

"Wow!" Sean replied.

"That was so cool!" said David.

"That was amazing!" Ashira commented.

Even Mr. Rosen was impressed.

"Can you teach us how to do that?" asked Sean.

"That is what I will be teaching you this year," replied Mr. Amadeus with a pleased smile.

Chapter 14 – P.E.

As they walked into the gym, David noticed right away that something seemed out of place.

"Mom, why are the soccer goals at the ceiling?" asked Ashira, looking up.

"Oh, that's for the more advanced students. Don't worry, you won't be starting up that high," Mrs. Rosen said reassuringly.

Sean and his parents walked into the gym as Mrs. Rosen had finished talking.

"What do you mean?" asked Sean.

Mrs. Rosen glanced at Mrs. Shaunessy, and then at Mr. Rosen. Mrs. Rosen was trying to decide how to answer the question, as she knew safety was very important to Mr. Rosen and she didn't want to worry him.

Mr. Rosen had relaxed in the astronomy room. It had seemed like an observatory to him, and he loved observatories. The music room had a different focus, but it was still music, and still wonderful. He even had enjoyed the art room. Herbs and spices making colors had sounded interesting to him. Not typically what an elementary school would teach, but not too different.

Even Mrs. Dray's class hadn't been what he had remembered from his childhood as third grade, but there was still reading, writing, math, science, and history, as Mrs. Dray had explained to him. The focus was a little less diversified, but all of the subjects were still there. He had tried to ignore the books soaring through the air toward their designated shelves in the library, as it was too much for his brain to comprehend.

"Well, children, the reason the goals are on the ceiling is because by fifth grade, or before, that's where you will be kicking the balls," Mrs. Rosen answered slowly.

"Honey, that's not feasible. They couldn't possibly kick soccer balls that high," Mr. Rosen protested.

"Dear, they aren't kicking them that high. They will be that high," stated Mrs. Rosen gently.

"What?!" exclaimed Mr. Rosen. He wasn't sure if he was excited to be able to watch a new sport, as he loved sports, or terrified at the thought of his children floating twenty feet in the air without a net anywhere in sight.

"In P.E., children, you will learn to levitate. That is, you will learn to push against the ground with your mind, in order to push your body up into the air," Mrs. Rosen explained.

Suddenly, a short, curly, dark-haired woman appeared dressed in work-out clothes.

"You must be here for Open House! How wonderful! My name is Coach Ricky Simmons. How great to meet you. I know we're all going to have fun this year!" she said energetically.

"Do you want to know the key to levitating? Well, you need to pump! That's it, pump! You can do it! It's like you're pumping air into a tire. Pump with your mind, push down against the floor, and soon you...will...be...levitating," cheered Coach Simmons, as she rose off the floor and into the air.

She snapped her fingers. A soccer ball appeared in her left hand. She dropped it in mid-air and kicked it straight into the goal on her right side.

"Wow!" said the children. Several more students had drifted into the gym to watch the Coach's demonstration. They were awed and amazed at what they would be learning in the coming year.

"When is the first day of school, again, Mom?" asked David, grinning. Sports were a comfort zone for him. Especially soccer.

"September 1st," replied his twin. "Not soon enough!" she said, her eyes shining in anticipation, remembering the art room and the different ways she could explore making colors and new forms of art.

Chapter 15 – First Day of School

"So, this is it?" said David, rocking back and forth on his heels as he stood waiting for the bus at the edge of their driveway. It was a foggy morning in Roswell, Georgia. Not quite as thick as pea soup, but almost. He couldn't see past the bushes on the far side of the house.

"This is what?" Ashira asked, looking up and down the street nervously, and only seeing fog.

"Our first day of school. I don't see why you didn't want Mom to be standing with us," he added to his sister, as he glanced back at the window and waved to their mother, who was watching them. She waved back at him.

David liked to have their mother nearby. Her presence made him feel safer. Ashira had always liked to be more independent. She was the one who didn't want their mother to walk them to class at school, she preferred to walk by herself or with a friend.

"She set up protective enchantments around us, so that no one can get to us. I think we'll be fine," Ashira said impatiently.

"But, what if it's the wrong bus?" David said nervously, his hand going to the blue crystal around his neck.

"It won't be," replied his sister confidently.

The Salem Academy bus appeared and opened its doors wide for the children to climb aboard.

David and Ashira weren't the first students on the bus. They sat down and put their backpacks on the seats next to them. The twins' backpacks were in their favorite colors with their initials, as it was the only thing they could have with them that wasn't in school colors.

Sean was the next bus stop, and he sat down next to David. They had been corresponding since Open House. Rebecca was one of the last stops. The girls had been talking almost daily on the phone as well.

"Are you scared?" asked Rebecca of Ashira. Rebecca seemed a little nervous herself.

David glanced at Sean. Neither of the boys were going to admit they were scared, especially in front of the girls.

"A little," admitted Ashira, fingering the lavender crystal necklace her mother had made her.

"Ooh, that's pretty!" Rebecca said admiringly. "Where did you get that?"

"My mom made it for me. She made David one as well," Ashira said. "Well, she gave us a choice of stones, and these were the ones which glowed for us."

"Really?" asked Sean, glancing at David.

David shrugged and pulled out his pale blue crystal necklace. He was hoping Sean thought it was cool, and not stupid or anything.

"That's really neat!" said Sean. "I have a crystal, too, but mine isn't on a necklace. Good idea!"

"Thanks," said David. "Are we there yet? Or, do we have more stops to make?"

The sky over the school was bright and sunny, as the marble buildings that made up the Salem Academy sparkled in the sunlight. The children climbed off the bus and walked into the Dragon Foyer. The fourth and fifth graders walked through the white dragon's picture without pausing. The third graders stopped and stared at the picture.

Mrs. Ball came out from behind her desk, took one of the third grader's hands, and walked through the picture. The rest followed.

As they passed the Third Grade West classroom, Sean peered inside. "Why aren't they in class yet?"

"They don't start for another few hours. Don't forget, western time zones are behind us, not ahead," added David, remembering his mother's explanation about the different time zones for the different classes. He loved math and playing with numbers. Time zones were all about numbers. How far ahead or behind one time zone was from another.

As the children were filing into the classroom, Mrs. Dray pointed out that they had assigned seating. "Go find your names on your desks, please, children. Quickly, as we don't have any time to waste."

All the desks were filled within a minute or two. David counted twenty seats and none of them were empty. On each desk was a small, lightweight, hardbound notebook.

"This morning, each and every one of you is going to create a Book of Shadows. Your Book of Shadows is your own personal spell book. You will keep this book with you during your time at this school."

"Mrs. Dray? What happens if I spill something on it?" David asked. He was always knocking over his water glass at home. He liked to joke and call himself his grandfather's apprentice, as his grandfather was legendary in the family for spilling containers of liquid.

"During lunch this afternoon, I am going to cast preventive spells, such as proofing against water and fire over each of your books," replied Mrs. Dray.

"How do we add more pages?" asked Ashira, as she opened her book.

"When you need more pages, there is a spell I can teach you," Mrs. Dray said with a smile. "Oh, and children, please print neatly so that you can read the spells you have written. If you can't read it, there is no point in writing it down," she added.

For Mrs. Dray, there was a place for everything, and everything needed to be in its place when doing magic. Magic needed to be orderly and be taken step by step.

Chapter 16 – The First Spell

"The first spell we're learning today is a "come to me" spell, or bringing spell. You are going to practice bringing an object to yourself. It is kind of like teaching a dog to 'come'. Instead, you will be training yourself to focus your magic on one specific object."

Mrs. Dray watched the students' faces. They glanced around at each other, trying to see if anyone else knew what they were doing.

"Some of you may wonder why I'm teaching you a spell first, before I teach you spell theory," began Mrs. Dray.

David didn't understand or care about the spell theory part of it. He wanted to do magic now.

"The answer is that I wanted to give you a basic spell with which to practice. Oh, and by practice, I mean only at school. You are not allowed to do magic outside of school until you are of age," added Mrs. Dray, "unless it is supervised by a parent in the privacy of your own home." She looked sharply around the room and added, "You are now part of the magical community. You must learn to take responsibility for yourselves, and your growing powers."

"How old do we have to be to perform magic in public?" asked Sean.

"You have to pass your basic sorcerer's tests, otherwise known as BST, which you take when you are sixteen, similar to a driving test in the nonmagical world. That gives you some freedom. You then study to take your advanced sorcerer's tests, otherwise known as AST, when you are eighteen," the teacher replied.

"What happens if you perform magic outside of school?" questioned one of the Sawyer twins.

"You would be brought to the Board of Magical Abuse, which is under the Department of Magic. The Department of Magic is part of the NSA, the National Security Agency, in the United States government."

There were surprised looks on most of the students' faces.

"Any other questions before we write down our first spell?" asked Mrs. Dray.

"Can we use a regular pencil?" asked Sean nervously.

"Yes," smiled Mrs. Dray. "As long as you can read it, you may use a pencil or a pen. Any other questions? No? Good. Now, copy the words I'm writing on the white board down on the first page of your Book of Shadows."

David glanced at the board, and then wrote as neatly as he could the words: *Come to me, I summon thee, with the power of the wind, fly over the earth, the air will bring thee to me, and do harm to none.*

All the students were writing slowly and as neatly as they could, trying not to make any errors as they wrote. They were still writing when Mrs. Dray said, "Who can tell me the different parts of the spell?"

Ashira's hand went into the air first. Mrs. Dray nodded at her to speak.

"First, we state the command, then state the power we are using to make the command work," said Ashira, a bit awkwardly.

"Very good! Ashira, is it? Good powers of reasoning, Ashira," exclaimed Mrs. Dray. "Now, children, take out your paper and your red folders, as you will want to take notes on what I am going to explain to you. We are discussing basic spell theory." She paused while everyone took out their red folders.

David remembered that the yellow folder was for Astronomy, the green folder was for herbs and plants, the brown folder was for animals, the red folder was for spell construction, and the blue folder was for history.

"In this spell, we used the powers of wind, earth, and air. You need to pull from a minimum of three forces of nature when you construct a spell," began Mrs. Dray.

"Why?" asked Sean.

"Good question. The answer is that you are pulling energies to create the power needed to perform the spell. When you are more advanced, you may not need to use as many energies." Mrs. Dray answered. "Can anyone name the other forces of nature?"

Half the class raised their hands. A boy named Parker was selected to answer first. "Sun," he said confidently.

Mrs. Dray nodded encouragingly and selected another student to add to the list.

"Water?" Rebecca said.

"Yes, very good," Mrs. Dray paused to look at the seating chart map on her desk, "Aidan Warren, what is the opposite of water?"

"Fire?" replied Aidan.

"Very good, everyone, very good," said the teacher. "Take out your crystals children. Did everyone remember to bring a crystal to class this morning? If you don't have your crystal with you, raise your hand."

Mrs. Dray walked around the class to see everyone's crystals. For those few who did not have a crystal, she brought each student up to her desk separately. Then she brought out a few crystals from one the drawers in her desk to see which one glowed in the student's hand. If none of the crystals glowed, the student was sent to the Dragon Foyer to see if there were any crystals in the lost and found which might work.

Mrs. Dray smiled approvingly at David's and Ashira's necklaces.

"Everyone unzip whatever part of your backpack that holds your snack. Now, I want each of you to picture in your mind what you brought for snack this morning. If you aren't sure, then check." She waited for the students to check their bags.

Chapter 17 – Snacks and Spells

"Take a deep breath, children, and picture your snack clearly in your mind. Now, hold your crystal and repeat the spell softly while you picture your snack," stated Mrs. Dray calmly.

The magic in the air intensified briefly, as everyone repeated the spell to themselves.

Ashira was fingering her necklace while she said the spell, and she was pleasantly surprised to see peanut butter crackers at her desk when she looked down.

"Excellent, Ashira! Excellent!" Mrs. Dray exclaimed.

Ashira beamed. Her twin frowned.

A few others had produced their snacks on their desks. "Don't worry, children, usually it takes several tries to..." Mrs. Dray's voice trailed off. She was standing directly in front of David's desk and staring mesmerized at an abnormally large egg sitting on top of it.

Mrs. Dray was trying hard to retain her composure in front of the children. She had a feeling about what was inside the egg.

The egg itself was at least a foot and half tall and a foot wide. David was staring at the egg as well with a shocked expression on his face.

"Mrs. D-dray? I don't know where it came from..." David began.

Mrs. Dray pursed her lips together and said, "Parker, go to the Dragon Foyer and tell Mrs. Ball to find Principal Powers immediately. Tell her I think we have a dragon egg. Go, now, Parker!"

The children looked to Mrs. Dray for guidance. She had seemed cheerful and structured, expecting everything, until now.

David stood up from his seat and backed a few feet away from his desk.

"I wish Mrs. Tres was here. She's seen more of these than I have, but Third Grade West doesn't begin for at least another hour," added Mrs. Dray. "Alright, everyone remain calm." She murmured a spell under her breath, and a crate with a large pillow inside appeared at the back of the classroom. She continued murmuring, while waving her hand. The egg floated inside the crate and landed gently on top of the plush pillow, as the door to the crate closed. The crate was against the far wall of the room behind the students' desks.

"You may sit down now, David," said Mrs. Dray distractedly.

David sat down immediately at his desk.

"Tell me what happened," Mrs. Dray said with a sigh.

David bit his lip as he answered her. "I held my crystal, said the spell, and then there was an egg on my desk. I promise!"

"What is your snack, David?" she asked matter-of-factly.

David reached into his backpack and pulled out a small blue oval container with two hard-boiled eggs inside. "They were leftover from our lunch yesterday. My mom said I should take them for snack."

"Thank you, David. No, you are not in trouble. Now we know that we are looking for a large blue oval container somewhere in this school which would have contained the egg. I'm sure I could bring the container to us, but that wouldn't tell us where it came from. I will have to do some scrying." She sighed again and began handing out textbooks.

"Children, open your textbook, Exploring Animals and Their Habitats. Please review the chapter on dragons while I speak with Director Powers. Please also make notes on the different kinds of dragons and their habitats. I will be back momentarily," said Mrs. Dray as she vanished out the door.

Parker came back into the room after notifying the principal. He wanted to know where the egg went. One of the children pointed it out to him at the back of the classroom. Most of the other students crowded around the crate to see what would happen.

David had already seen the egg up close, so he stayed at his desk and chatted with Sean. Sean had seen the egg when it had arrived on David's desk, but he still kept craning his neck to see more of it. He stayed at David's desk to keep his friend company. David wanted to keep as much room between himself and the egg as possible, as he was freaked out that on his first day of school, something weird had happened to him.

Ashira and Rebecca wandered over, holding the animal habitat textbook.

"It says in here that there are nine different kinds of dragons. The color of the dragon tells you what powers it has and where it lives," began Ashira.

"That's really neat," said David, opening his textbook. A textbook dragon sounded cool. He wasn't so sure about a live one. Maybe if he learned more about dragons, they wouldn't be quite so scary, or so large.

"Wow! Red dragons live around the Volcanic Ring area and breathe lava, orange dragons live in the plains and breathe fire, yellow dragons live in the rain forest and breathe lightning..."

"This is so cool!" said Sean, as he continued where David had left off. "Green dragons live in the Australian swamp lands and breathe acid, blue dragons live in the ocean and breathe flooding water, gray dragons live in the forest regions and breathe thunder, brown dragons live in the desert and breathe smoke... well, that explains dust storms..."

"You forgot that black dragons live in the Amazon jungle and breathe poison, and white dragons live in the polar regions and breathe ice," Rebecca added, flipping the pages of the book.

"What about the color of the egg? Does that tell us anything?" asked David, trying to see the egg from where he was sitting.

Chapter 18 – The Egg

"The book talks more about where to find dragons, what they eat, how their features are different depending on where they live, and how toxic their breath is to us," said Ashira skimming the text. "The eggs usually have a tint which would tell us which color it is. What color is the egg?"

"White, I think," replied David, peering at the crate.

"What does toxic mean?" asked Rebecca, twisting her hair around her finger into a tiny curl.

"Dangerous and deadly," answered David, wondering if he could sit at the teacher's desk until she came back.

"Are the babies toxic?" asked Sean nervously, thinking that the four of them really should move closer to the other side of the room.

"No, thank goodness," Ashira replied, studying the text. She fidgeted with her hair bow.

Mrs. Ball walked into the classroom. "Children, please take your seats, now. Thank you. Your teacher will be back in a few minutes..." began Mrs. Ball. She exuded an air of peacefulness and serenity.

"Is the egg dangerous?" asked Lily Heschel.

"No. Dragon eggs are not dangerous to the touch, which is why Mrs. Dray decided to leave it in the classroom," explained Mrs. Ball.

"What if it hatches?" asked Noah Sawyer.

"I doubt it's going to hatch, dear. Baby dragons are not dangerous to humans. Although, when it hatches, it will be hungry," Mrs. Ball said with a smile.

"Does it eat humans?" asked Aidan.

"No. Baby dragons do not eat humans. I see Mrs. Dray has passed out your animal habitats books. Can anyone tell me what baby dragons eat?" asked Mrs. Ball.

Ashira raised her hand. "It depends on what kind of baby dragon. Most of them eat fish as babies, except for the

African Desert dragons which eat birds since there aren't fish in the desert."

"Very good," smiled Mrs. Ball. "My husband worked with dragons when we were first married."

"What kind of dragons?" asked one of the boys.

"National Forest dragons. They're gray in color. The babies can produce a noise similar to thunder from a storm. The really powerful adult gray dragons can produce a sonic boom. The gray dragons have an extra lining in their throats to be able to do that, and they even have a bit of webbing on their feet for catching fish in the nearby rivers. Ear protection is required when you work with them," she told the class.

"Where were you?" asked Nick Wall.

"Yellowstone National Park," Mrs. Ball replied. "All dragons are nocturnal, meaning they are awake during the night and sleep during the day. They sleep in caves. They are also omnivorous, meaning they eat both meat and plants."

"Did your husband work with any other kinds of dragons?" asked Zachary.

Mrs. Ball smiled and shook her head.

There was a strange cracking noise which echoed in the room.

"It can't be cracking," said Mrs. Ball. "That isn't possible," she added shocked, as she walked to the back of the room. "This can't be happening on the first day of school..."

She took a deep breath and turned around. She pointed at two students. The first one was Michael Ashbrooke. She handed him a hall pass which was a metal number three. "Go to the Dragon Foyer and tell Mrs. Cards that the dragon is hatching now. Run, please, but carefully."

Mrs. Ball turned to Hannah Lacefield and handed her another hall pass which was a Salem Academy placard. "Go to the cafeteria and ask them if they have any fresh fish or chicken. Preferably raw. We need at least a couple of pounds. Tell them I sent you. Quickly, thank you."

Mrs. Ball turned back to the egg. "I don't see any tinting, which means that either the dragon is less powerful, or it will be a one of the lighter colored baby dragons, such as gray, white, baby blue, or pale yellow. Orange, green, red, black, or brown would definitely tint the shell." She sighed in relief and turned back to the class. "We already discussed the National Forest dragons. Who can tell me about the other lighter colored dragons?"

David raised his hand. "The Rainforest dragons are yellow in color. They have an extra stomach to process wood and turn it into energy to make lightning. They also have a little bit of webbing on their feet to adapt to rainwater. It says here that the babies eat fish, and the adults eat snakes, sloths, birds, and other animals."

Lily Heschel raised her hand. "There are also the Oceanic dragons, divided into the Atlantic and Pacific. The babies eat fish and are light blue. The adults turn a darker, deeper blue and eat larger ocean creatures, such as sharks. They have extra webbing on their feet and their wings for swimming in the ocean. They have an extra stomach to store the water they use as a defense to drown their predators."

Chapter 19 – More About Dragons

"Very good class. There is one you haven't mentioned. The Polar Ice dragons. They are white and live in the polar regions. They have an extra stomach to process the water around them and freeze it into ice and snow. They have some extra webbing on their feet and wings for swimming in the ocean. They also have huge layers of blubber to protect them against the severe cold in the polar regions. The babies eat fish and the adults eat sharks and other regional animals."

"Have you ever seen a baby dragon being born, Mrs. Ball?" asked one of the girls.

"Yes, I have. Baby dragons have pale, shiny scales which are very thin. As they get older, their scales thicken and deepen in color and luster. An old dragon will have scales which resemble jewels, such as rubies, emeralds, and sapphires, which is why they are hunted. Dragon scales are worth quite a bit. Of course, most hunters don't survive an encounter with an ancient dragon," said Mrs. Ball.

"Why not?" asked one of the students.

"Their scales are too thick to penetrate. They are very powerful as well," she replied.

Hannah arrived back from the cafeteria, holding a large container of raw fish in one hand, with the Salem Academy placard underneath it, and holding her nose with the other hand. Hannah put her hall pass back on Mrs. Dray's desk. "The fish smells, Mrs. Ball."

Mrs. Ball took the container from Hannah and thanked her. She placed the fish next to the crate in the back of the room. She surveyed the cracking shell and pursed her lips. "Children, I don't want to move the egg at this point as I don't want to harm the baby dragon inside. A baby blue dragon would get you a little wet, which is no big deal. A baby gray would make some noise, but it would be so pretty, children. They look almost silver as babies. I'm most worried about a baby yellow dragon, as it would tend to send off sparks, which could be dangerous."

"What about the white dragons, Mrs. Ball?" asked one of the boys.

Crack, crackle, crack, snap...

Mrs. Ball watched the egg tensely and glanced at the door to see if Mrs. Dray or Director Powers was there yet. The egg began violently rolling back and forth.

"All students, come to the front of the room immediately!" said Mrs. Ball tensely.

Mrs. Dray walked in the room, followed by Director Powers, as a small pale snout appeared. The snout was followed by two little arms as the head thrust its way out of its shell. The class gasped collectively.

Mrs. Ball breathed a sigh of relief as the baby Polar Ice dragon emerged from its shell. She murmured something, waved her hand, and a bowl with fresh cold water appeared in the dragon's crate. Then, she waved her hand again, and the pieces of fish floated in the air towards the baby white dragon's open mouth.

After the baby dragon had finished the fish and slurped some water with its long pink tongue, it emitted a large burp containing snowflakes, burying several nearby desks in snow.

"Wow! That's cool!" said one of the students.

The little dragon giggled, emitting a few more piles of snowflakes right outside its crate at the back of the room. Then it sighed sleepily, lay down with a WHUF, as cold air flooded the room, and began snoring lightly.

"It's so cute!" chimed many of the girls. Although all the students huddled together for several more minutes, trying to regain some warmth.

Mrs. Dray murmured something and waved her hand in the air. The snow vanished from the desks. "Clearly, we have to move it, before the rest of the room is covered in snow," she said to Director Powers appealingly.

"Maybe Coach Simmons would be gracious enough to lend us some of her space for a day or two, until we find out from where the egg came and what to do with it. We need a cool area," said Director Powers, as she stepped out of the classroom to consult with Coach Simmons.

"Mrs. Dray? If dragons are descended from lizards, how can they survive in the cold, especially in the polar regions?" asked Rebecca.

"Gigantothermy," Mrs. Dray answered. "Part of the chapter on dragons mentions it. I'll give you a brief overview while we are waiting to warm up. Gigantothermy states that greater volume to surface area ratio. In other words, the larger the animal, the smaller the surface area to get cold. When an animal in a polar region moves, its body uses energy to provide heat. Therefore larger reptiles gain heat faster than they lose it, and it is easier for them to maintain a high constant body temperature. Plus, the Polar Ice dragons have lots of blubber to insulate them."

Chapter 20 – More Eggs

Mrs. Dray paused when Director Powers entered the room.

"Coach Simmons said we could use part of the gym as a habitat for the baby dragon today. She was planning on teaching outside this afternoon anyway. I created the habitat before coming back here."

Director Powers looked thoughtful for a moment. "Crystal, will you please move the crate down to the habitat with me? Helen, I'll let you know if there are any other updates."

Mrs. Ball murmured something and waved her hands toward the crate, as if to guide the dragon's crate over the children's heads and down the hall to the gymnasium.

"Thank you for not panicking class," said Mrs. Dray. "You may all take your seats now." She looked at David thoughtfully. "David, if you don't mind, would you please repeat the spell you said when you tried to bring your snack to your desk, while you hold your crystal again? I want to see if anything else turns up. Director Powers and I didn't have luck scrying for any large blue oval container which held the dragon egg."

David took a deep breath, closed his eyes, and said the spell. Everyone in the class watched. He opened his eyes to see another egg on his desk. This one was about the same size as the first, except the egg was a little darker.

Mrs. Dray put her hand on David's shoulder. "It's okay, David. I asked you to do this. Hannah, please take a hall pass and go back to the cafeteria and ask for another couple of pounds of fish. Parker, please take a hall pass and go tell Mrs. Ball that we have another egg."

Mrs. Dray created another crate with pillows, and floated the egg into it.

"David, try again, please," said Mrs. Dray.

Another egg appeared on David's desk. This one was the same size as the others, but was pinkish in tint.

Mrs. Dray created a second crate in the room with pillows, and floated the pinkish egg into it. She pursed her lips and floated the crate with the pinkish egg over the children's heads and down the hall. She came back a minute later.

"Sorry, children. That last egg was most likely a red dragon. They produce lava. Having a bit of snow in the class is fun. Having lava melt everything is not. Plus, I have been told that red dragons tend to be a little cranky," Mrs. Dray turned to David. "I'm sorry to have to ask you this, David. But please try one more time for me. Don't worry, I think this time will be safer."

David tried again and was relieved to see his hard-boiled chicken's egg sitting on his desk. He breathed a sigh of relief.

"Yes, that's what I thought would happen," said Mrs. Dray. "You have, completely accidentally, intercepted someone's research project, I believe."

"A research project?" repeated David in a confused tone.

"The first egg was a Polar Ice dragon, a white dragon. The third egg was most likely a Volcanic Ring dragon, which is a red dragon. Which means, the second egg would be a..." said Mrs. Dray, prompting someone in the class to finish her sentence. "Can anyone guess what the second egg probably is?"

Ashira raised her hand. "A National Forest dragon? A gray one? For the colors of the school?"

"Good deductive reasoning, Ashira," Mrs. Dray said.

Rebecca first turned white as a sheet of paper, then blushed bright red. "Mrs. Dray? May I be excused for a minute?"

Mrs. Dray looked puzzled, but handed Rebecca the remaining hall pass, which was a little metal statue of a dragon sitting on a crystal ball.

Director Powers walked back into the classroom with Mrs. Ball. "I heard you had another egg, Helen," said the director.

"Two, actually, Wilhelmina. I let this one stay, as I think it's a National Forest dragon. I had to move the last one, as I believe it's a Volcanic Ring dragon, and I wasn't going to risk exposing them to that. Too dangerous. Coach Simmons promised she would set up a habitat for the red dragon, and for this one as well," said Mrs. Dray, referring to the egg in the classroom.

Mrs. Ball walked over to the dragon's egg at the back of the classroom. "From my limited experience, it looks like a National Forest dragon egg. I wouldn't swear to it, mind you, but it..."

The egg began rocking back and forth violently in its crate at the back of the room. Several cracks appeared all over the egg. The children stood up from their seats again and went to the front of the classroom.

"Wilhelmina, I believe this is a research project of some sort. It's too much of a coincidence to have a white, a gray, and a red dragon, when those are our mascots for the school," said Mrs. Dray to Director Powers.

Chapter 21 – Three Dragons, Three Colors

"I agree. It's too deliberate for a practical joke. No student would bring in dragon eggs for a project with the risk of getting expelled, without getting my approval. I don't recall seeing anything come across my desk about dragon eggs. That, I would have remembered!" insisted Director Powers.

A silver snout appeared out of the bits of cracked eggshell. The class was awed by it.

Hannah had arrived a few minutes earlier with the fish, and was grateful not to be sent on a third mission to get fish for the Volcanic Ring dragon in the gymnasium. Mrs. Dray sent a note to the lunchroom staff, asking them to deliver it themselves.

As little silver arms were appearing out of the wreckage of the shell, Rebecca arrived with an older student and one of the high school teachers.

Director Powers raised her eyebrows at the sight of one of her high school teachers in the elementary school wing. "Ms. Scienza? Would you care to explain the presence of dragon eggs in my school?"

"Director Powers, I handed you the paperwork for Jack Montgomery's science project over the summer to study live baby dragons in their own habitats. You approved it. I have to admit, I was, well, somewhat surprised, but, it was your decision," Ms. Scienza answered.

"Three eggs, tricolor eggs..." the director's eyes went wide. "I didn't think he was talking about **real** dragon eggs!" She sighed. "That's why you enclosed several pages about habitats being required. Although, from the paperwork, I was under the impression that your class was going to build the habitats themselves," said Director Powers, eyeing Ms. Scienza coldly.

"Yes, well, the eggs evidently hatched before we were ready. I was under the impression that the eggs weren't due to hatch for another few weeks, at least..." trailed off Ms. Scienza.

"Didn't anyone ever tell you that the more you move the eggs at the end of their cycle, the quicker they hatch?" asked Mrs. Ball shrewdly. "Especially when you summon them. It shreds their outer core, prompting them to ready themselves to leave the egg."

"I strongly suggest you survey what available room there is in the high school wing for the habitats, and get back with me in the next hour. We want to make Coach Simmons happier by removing the dragons from her gym," said Director Powers.

"Of course, Director Powers, of course," replied Ms. Scienza quickly.

Jack looked longingly at the silver baby dragon. "Do you mind if I feed it?" he asked Mrs. Dray.

Mrs. Dray smiled and said, "Go right ahead."

Jack waved his right hand in the air and floated pieces of fish towards the silver dragon's waiting mouth. After it had been fed, the little dragon screwed up its face, as if it was going to sneeze, and let out a shattering thunder clap.

Everyone in the class jumped. Several screamed, including Mrs. Dray. Mrs. Ball smiled and said it reminded her of her honeymoon in Yellowstone National Park.

The silver baby dragon had a satisfied and dignified look on its face as it surveyed the room after emitting its noise, circled in its crate five times, laid down, and snored. Its snores sounded like the gentle rumblings of the beginning of a thunderstorm.

"That was the best first day of school, ever!" said David to Sean. David decided he wasn't afraid of the baby dragons, at least not while they were safe in their habitats.

Sean nodded in agreement. To have seen two dragons born! What a day!

They were sitting on the Salem Academy bus, waiting for the doors to close for the ride home.

The rest of the day had passed smoothly enough. Ms. Scienza had evidently found room in the high school wing of the school, and had some of her students spend the rest of the day preparing three different habitats for the baby dragons. When she came back into their room to remove the National Forest baby dragon at the end of the day, she let the class know that they would be able to view all the dragons next week when they became acclimated to their new surroundings.

Mrs. Dray clarified this statement by adding that viewing the dragons would mean seeing them through a barrier, especially the Volcanic Ring dragon.

The rest of the day had been merely an introduction to the different textbooks and to the basic steps of levitation. It had been unlike any other physical education class any of them had ever had. Although, in between trying to focus their mental energies to pushing against the ground, the students had taken turns playing soccer on the ground.

Ashira sat down next to her brother and gestured to Rebecca to join them. "How did you know about the eggs?" she asked Rebecca.

"My dad works with dragons. He doesn't work in the field as much as he used to, but I remember Jack, my brother, boasting all summer about his science project and how it was going to be the best ever. I remember my dad telling Jack that he had to be responsible and that this was very serious stuff. All the little details I had heard, pieced themselves together after I saw all three eggs and Mrs. Dray talk about intercepting someone's research project. I figured that Jack was either behind it, or knew something about it," said Rebecca.

"Which one was your favorite?" asked Ashira. The dragon babies were cuter than she had imagined. They had also been more powerful than she had expected, but then, so had school.

"I wish we had a chance to see the Volcanic Ring dragon hatch," said Sean. "That would have been so cool! I mean, lava!"

"Yeah," agreed David. "But, the silver one was really neat, especially after Jack fed it and it opened its mouth. That was the loudest noise I have ever heard from something that small before!"

"I liked the white one," Rebecca said shyly. She was softer spoken than Ashira. "Little snowflakes everywhere. It giggled. It was adorable! What about you, Ashira? Which one was your favorite?"

"I don't know. The silver one was so pretty, but so loud! The amount of snow from the white baby dragon amazed me. If this is what the babies are like, I now understand why Mrs. Ball said that hunters who try to kill the ancient ones for their scales rarely survive," Ashira commented. She looked thoughtful.

"I can't wait to tell my parents about school!" said Sean.

"Oh, no!" Ashira exclaimed.

"What's wrong?" asked Rebecca.

Ashira and David exchanged glances and then said in unison, "What are we going to tell our Dad?!"

ABOUT THE AUTHOR

Lisa B. Diamond lives in Georgia with her husband, Richard, and their two children. She is currently hard at work on *The Salem Academy for Young Sorcerers, Book 10*.

Her books are on sale on Amazon in Kindle (ebook) and paperback format.